Edward Zlotkowski

Badger and Fox

& friends

Illustrated by

Karen Busch Holman

For Ruby and Micah

The Big Puzzle

"Hey, Fox," Badger asked, putting down her book, "do you know how many stars there are in the sky?"

"I never counted," Fox replied. "Do you know how many minutes there are until supper?"

"It's only mid-afternoon," Badger answered, looking at a clock on the wall. "Are you already hungry?"

"No," said Fox, "I'm bored. I wish it weren't so cold and we could go outside and have some fun."

"Well," said Badger, "I hope you find some fun things to do here in the den because we still have a lot of winter left."

"Hey," Fox suddenly cried, "you like to make puzzles. Want to make one?"

"Sure," Badger replied. "Let's make the big animal puzzle. That's my favorite."

"That one's pretty hard," Fox hesitated.

"It is," Badger admitted, "but it's great seeing the animals together."

✻

So Fox went to get the puzzle box while Badger cleared off the kitchen table. Fox opened the box and turned it over. A jumble of pieces fell out. "Wow!" she exclaimed. "There really are a lot of pieces!"

"We should have a strategy," Badger suggested. "What do you think?"

"Sure," said Fox. "Look, I already put together two pieces with black and white stripes. I bet it's the zebra."

✻

"It could be the skunk," Badger noted. "That's why we should have a strategy…"

"Hey, but look at this over here," Fox interrupted. "I just found two parts of the yellow lion… and here's another!"

"Pretty good," said Badger in surprise. "Maybe we don't need a strategy."

"It's up to you," Fox said, putting together three more pieces.

✻

It took the two friends two snacks and an hour before the puzzle was almost complete. Only ten, nine, eight, seven, six and five, four, three, two pieces left and…

and…"Hey," said Fox, "One piece is missing."

"Did it fall on the floor?" Badger asked.

Fox checked. "Nope, not on the floor."

"It's not still in the box?"

"Nope."

"Not on our laps?"

"Not on mine."

"Then I guess we need to make a thorough search," Badger decided.

"Or we could just have another snack and look for it some other time. We don't really need it to see the picture. It's definitely part of the alligator's tail," Fox pointed out.

"No," Badger insisted. "I think we should look for it now. After all, the puzzle isn't really complete until – until it's complete!"

"How about another snack," Fox again suggested.

But by now Badger was walking across the den towards her bed.

Everything around the bed was very tidy, and the bed itself was neatly made. All of her clothing was stored in a bureau with three drawers and most of her

things were arranged on a set of shelves against the wall – two shelves for books, a shelf for containers filled with crayons, pencils, and pieces of chalk, and a low shelf for the games and puzzles the two friends shared. Nearby were two boxes – one for puppets and one for everything else.

❄

It was to the "everything else" box that Badger now made her way and fished out a tan explorer's hat. "There – that should help," she said, putting the hat on and glancing at herself in a mirror.

"Hey," said Fox, "that's a good idea," and a few seconds later she too had some dress-up help in the form of a Super Fox cape. "Now we can find anything!" she said.

❄

"Okay," Badger announced. "The first thing we should do is look to see if the missing piece was put by mistake in another puzzle box."

"You mean, we have to make all these puzzles?" Fox sounded alarmed.

"No, just look for a small piece of green alligator. Some puzzles have only big pieces or pieces with completely different kinds of shapes or colors. It shouldn't be that hard to spot a piece from another puzzle. Besides," Badger explained, "the harder puzzles usually tell you on the box how many pieces there are, so you can just count the pieces."

"Sounds like fun," Fox frowned as she began searching through the puppet box.

"Hey," Badger cried. "We're supposed to be looking for the missing puzzle piece."

"I know, I know," Fox said. "I'm just getting a few puppets to help us."

Badger began checking the puzzle boxes while Fox put a hedgehog puppet on one paw and a duck puppet on the other.

"You silly duck," Fox made the hedgehog say, *"don't you know the difference between a puppet and a puzzle?"*

"Don't be so prickly, Hedgehog," Fox made the duck reply. *"I'm doing the best I can. Besides, there's this enormous badger taking up all the space and emptying puzzle boxes all over the floor. What do you think we should do about her?"*

"Well," said the hedgehog, *"first we need a strategy."*

"What kind of a strategy?" the duck asked.

"A strategy to get another snack," the hedgehog replied.

Meanwhile Badger went carefully from puzzle to puzzle looking for the missing piece. After putting all the pieces of the last puzzle back in their box, she gave a big sigh. "Well," she said, looking very serious, "it's not here. That means we lost it somewhere else. Fox, do you remember where we last made the animal puzzle?" Before Fox could reply, Badger answered her own question, "Oh, I remember. We made it a few weeks ago over by your bed!"

They both looked over at Fox's bed. It had not been made, and it was covered with – among other things – her guitar, two dirty plates, a big pad of paper, a ball, a brush, several t-shirts, a pair of running shoes, and an empty box of crackers. Badger looked at Fox and sighed. Fox looked at Badger and smiled. "Kinda messy," Fox said.

"Kinda," Badger agreed.

❅

"Maybe we should just have another snack," Fox suggested.

"C'mon," said Badger, crossing the den to Fox's bed. "I'm sure we'll find the piece if we look hard enough. – Besides, if we straighten up around your bed, you'll have more room for your snowshoes."

"What snowshoes?" Fox asked with a confused look. "I don't have any snowshoes…", but Badger had already gone over to Fox's bed and was busy picking things up and sorting through the piles of clothing that lay on the floor.

❅

"Hey, what's this?" Badger suddenly asked, holding up a book buried at the bottom of one of Fox's piles. "It's my animal encyclopedia. I was wondering what happened to it."

"Oh, right," said Fox a little awkwardly. "I wanted to check something."

"Maybe you should check and see if it says anything about foxes being messy," Badger suggested.

❅

"Let me see," cried Fox, snatching the book. "Okay, right here – **FOX**. It says: *The fox is probably the most intelligent of all animals. It can escape even from very difficult situations. It can run incredibly fast and is unbelievably cute.*"

"Wait a minute!" Badger shouted. "It doesn't say that. Let me see."

"No, it does say that," Fox laughed and held the book back out of Badger's reach.

❄

"Fox," said Badger, "give me my book or I'm going to tickle you!"

"No!" Fox shrieked as Badger pounced on her and began to tickle her.

But Badger wouldn't stop, so Fox dropped the book and began to tickle Badger.

"No you don't!" shouted Badger and hit Fox with a pillow.

"Aha!" Fox shouted back, "a pillow fight! Remember, you started it!" and she grabbed a pillow of her own and started hitting Badger.

❄

The pillow fight was great fun, and neither Badger nor Fox wanted to stop. Finally, however, they got too tired to go on and both fell back on the bed laughing and gasping for breath.

"Good fight!" said Fox, hitting Badger with her pillow one last time.

"Good fight," agreed Badger, "but we still haven't found the missing piece, and it's starting to get late.

We should make supper soon."

"Sounds good to me," said Fox.

❄

They both got up from the bed and returned to the table where the big animal puzzle was still incomplete.

"I hate to give up," Badger sighed. She picked up the cover of the box and looked at the picture. Then she started tapping on the picture of the alligator. "Right here, right here is where…" and incredibly – Plop – right in the middle of the puzzle fell the missing piece!

❄

"Now how did that happen?" Badger asked picking up the piece. "Hey, look," she suddenly cried. "In the back there's a sticky red spot. One of us must have been eating jelly the last time we made the puzzle and some jelly got stuck here. Then the piece got stuck on the bottom of the cover!"

"Don't look at me," Fox said. "I only eat chocolate when I'm making puzzles." Both of them laughed. Then Fox added, "But I hope something else gets lost tomorrow. This was fun!"

The Spectacular Snowbank

"Brrrrr," said Fox, pulling a blanket around herself even more tightly, "This is the coldest winter ever! Even my tail feels cold."

Badger poked her head out of the door of their den. "Fox, come, look!" she called excitedly. Fox hurried to look. She let out a long OOOOOOOOOOOOOOOO which turned into a happy Yip Yip Yip Yip Yip Yip Yip which turned into a crazy eee eee eee eee eeeee. Badger covered her ears and Fox started to dance.

❆

It had snowed all night, and in the bright morning sun, the two friends completely forgot about the cold. It was, they agreed, the perfect day to play outside. Quickly they pulled on their red snowsuits, their yellow snow boots, their blue mittens, and their purple hats. They gathered together a small shovel, a snow shovel, a carrot, several big buttons, an old hat, an old scarf, a broom, and two sleds. Then they were ready to go out.

❄

The snow was deep and thick and the whitest white they had ever seen. Badger lay down on her back and moved her arms and legs up and down to make a snow bird. Fox did the same. Then Badger made another, and another, and Fox made another, and another, and still another. – Soon the snow everywhere around their den was covered with snow birds, and they might have made even more when something suddenly caught their attention.

❄

A little ways away, at the bottom of a hill, lay a spectacular snowbank. It was so deep they couldn't wade through it. In fact, they could barely touch its top with the end of their snow shovel. For several minutes they just stood there, looking at it in amazement. Finally, Badger said, "Fox, are you thinking what I'm thinking."

"You bet," said Fox. "Let's make a snow house!"

❄

At the same moment, they spotted Otter and Raccoon pushing through the snow at the top of the hill. Every few steps they would stop and throw snowballs at each other. When they noticed Badger and Fox, they waved.

"Hey, guys," Badger called, "Want to make a snow house?"

"Sure!" they called back. "Sounds like fun." And with that Otter flopped down on his tummy, Raccoon climbed up on Otter's back and the two of them slid down the hill.

"Okay," Badger asked, "What kind of a snow house do we want to make? How big should it be? Should it have windows? Should it be square or round?" But before anyone could answer, Fox had already grabbed the shovel and was using it to pack down the sides of the snowbank. Then she threw more snow onto the sides and packed them down again. Since Fox seemed to know what she was doing, the others simply followed her example.

Little by little something sort of like an igloo began to take shape. "I thought this would be much easier to do," Fox panted. "I'm just glad you guys came by to help," she added, looking at Otter and Raccoon.

"Do you think the walls are strong enough for us to hollow out the inside?" Badger asked when they finally stepped back to look at their work.

"Maybe we can test them," Raccoon suggested.

At this point, who should appear but Squirrel! "Hi, Squirrel," they all called. "Guess what? We're making a snow house!" Squirrel scampered lightly over the snow and leaped up onto the roof.

"What a great idea!" she cried, looking around at what they had done.

"Want to help?" Raccoon asked. "We need to test the walls."

"Sure," Squirrel answered. "Just tell me what to do."

So they gave Squirrel the small shovel and told her to check all over for soft spots. Then, wherever she found one, Fox or Raccoon would add more snow. Meanwhile, Badger and Otter dug a tunnel into the mound so they could hollow out the inside. It wasn't hard to dig the tunnel, but it took a lot of work to make enough room inside for all five of them.

Finally, when the snow house was finished, they crawled in. "Wow," whispered Squirrel, "This is incredible!" Everyone got very quiet. The outside light passing through the snow walls made the air inside seem blue. Everything felt magical and very, very special, and for a while no one said a word.

Then, as the cold began creeping up around them, Fox shivered and stuttered, "I think my tail is starting to freeze."

"Let's go have some hot cider," Badger suggested, and everyone cheered.

❄

"So, what do you think?" Badger asked as she put out a plate of cookies to go with the cider. "What should we do with our snow house?"

Raccoon suggested it would make a good hideout, and Otter thought they could use it as a fort for snowball fights. "How about using it to store things?" Badger asked.

"What kinds of things?" Raccoon wanted to know. No one said anything else for a long time.

❄

Finally, Squirrel jumped up. "I've got it! I've got it!" she cried, leaping up onto the back of her chair. "You know, just this morning I was talking to Owl," she explained, "and he said some of the birds couldn't find enough food because it's been so cold and snowy. So…"

Squirrel paused and jumped over to the back of Badger's chair. Then she continued with a big smile, "So, what if we used our snow house to store bird food?" And she twitched her tail back and forth in excitement.

❄

When the others still looked puzzled, she jumped over to the back of Fox's chair. "Listen," she said, "we started with a snowbank which we turned into a snow house. Why not turn the snow house into a food bank – a bird food bank?! Don't you see? We can bring in food through the tunnel, and, after we make a few windows, the birds can fly in through them whenever they want food. The roof and walls will keep the food from getting covered or blowing away. Don't you see, it's perfect!"

❄

Squirrel's enthusiasm was catchy, and the more the friends talked about turning the snowbank into a bird food bank, the more excited they became. Badger got out a pad of paper. "So, what do we need to do?" she asked.

"We need to make windows," Fox said.

"And we need to collect food," Otter added.

"And we need to let the birds know," Raccoon said and then asked, "By the way, what exactly do birds like to eat?"

❄

"I'll check with Owl," Squirrel answered. "He knows everything about birds."

"Great!" cried the others.

"And when we know what birds like to eat, I'll make a shopping list we can share with all our friends," Badger offered.

"Hey," Otter suggested, "if we tie boxes on our sleds, we can use them to collect the food."

"Good idea," said Badger. "I think we have a plan."

And indeed they did. Squirrel spoke to Owl who told her there were many foods birds liked to eat. Squirrel told Badger and Badger made a list: breakfast cereals, cut up fruits, raisins, sunflower seeds, dried corn, rice, pieces of bread, and a special favorite – peanut butter.

"What a great list!" Fox cried. "Peanut butter is also one of my favorites." So Badger and Fox again put on their red snowsuits, their yellow snow boots, their blue mittens, and their purple hats, and took the list around to all their friends.

Meanwhile, Squirrel leapt from tree to tree to tree, spreading the news. Soon, there was hardly a furry or a feathered animal in the forest that didn't know there would soon be a food bank to help the birds through the winter. All the friends worked hard. Hour after hour you could see them pulling their sleds from den to den, filling with food the boxes tied on top.

A few days later the food bank had more than enough food. Fox cut several windows in the walls, and birds started flying in and out almost at once. At the same time, many other animals came by to say hello and to see how they could help. Since the food bank was so close to Badger and Fox's den, they soon got to know dozens and dozens of new birds. Not only that, but from that point on, they awoke each morning to a chorus of beautiful bird song.

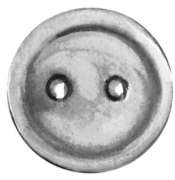

The Scary Shortcut

Early one day Badger and Fox decided to go on an adventure. Fox thought it would be fun to go somewhere unusual and suggested they go to the ocean. Badger said she thought the ocean was a good idea, but they should wait until they practiced their swimming a little. Then Badger suggested they explore the big hill on the other side of the river. Fox thought that would also be a good adventure.

Badger made a list of all the things they should take with them. She read the list to Fox. "First we need a map – like the map from our Treasure Island board game. Then we need some string in case we have to make something and a box of crayons in case we want to draw something. What do you think?"

"That sounds good to me," Fox answered, "But what about lunch?"

"Oh, right," Badger shook her head, "I almost forgot."

Badger made two peanut butter and jelly sandwiches and put them in her backpack. She also took two apples and a little bag of walnuts. Fox found a chocolate bar she had lost. Then they decided each should bring a kazoo in case they needed to frighten away something scary. Finally they left a note on the door of their den: *We are out on an adventure. Please come back tomorrow.*

Crossing the river was easy because there were places where it wasn't very deep and there were lots of rocks to hop across on. "C'mon, Fox," Badger called as Fox began hopping upstream from rock to rock just to see how far she could go. But Fox was already too far away to hear, so Badger had to chase after her hopping from rock to rock herself. It was so much fun, Badger forgot to be annoyed.

*

Finally they ran out of rocks and finished crossing to the other side of the river. "That's a big hill," Fox sighed, looking up, "more like a mountain if you ask me." They decided now was a good time for a snack and ate one of the apples as well as the chocolate bar. Then they set out to climb the hill. Higher and higher they climbed. "I think it's getting colder," Badger noted.

"I think so too," Fox agreed. "Maybe there will still be snow on top, and we can make a snow fox and a snow badger!"

On top there was no snow, but there was wind, and as it blew through some tall pine trees, it made a kind of eerie breathing sound or, when it blew stronger, a moaning and a groaning sound. "Badger, do you think there are ghosts up here?" Fox asked, taking her kazoo from her pocket just in case.

"I think ghosts only come out at night," Badger replied, also taking a kazoo from her pocket.

After a while they wandered down the back side of the hill and the spooky sounds stopped. They found a little path and wondered who had made it. "Let's see where this path goes," Fox suggested. And the two friends became so interested in following the winding path, they didn't notice it led to the bottom of a grassy slope. In the slope was a cave.

"Fox," Badger said, suddenly stopping and grabbing her friend's arm, "look, a cave!" For several minutes they just stood there staring at the dark opening. "I'm not sure but I think I just saw something move," Badger whispered.

"Maybe it's a friendly bear," Fox suggested.

"Or an unfriendly bear," Badger worried.

Together they tiptoed to the front of the cave. "I had an uncle who lived in a cave," Fox started to say, but Badger was listening for cave sounds.

"Maybe a hungry mountain lion lives there," she worried. "Or a fierce dragon," she added, grabbing Fox's arm. All of a sudden there was a rustling sound from somewhere in the cave.

Both friends again took out their kazoos and this time they brought them to their mouth. Then, just as they were about to let out a terrifying – or terrified – brrrrrrrrrrzzzzzzz, a little rat stuck its head out into the sunlight. He blinked a few times at the brightness, sat up on his hind legs, and said admiringly to Badger, "Those are very nice buttons on your overalls – very, very shiny. Mind if I take a look?"

Badger and Fox let out a big sigh of relief. They put away their kazoos, and the rat scurried over to look at the shiny buttons. "Those certainly are nice buttons," he repeated with a smile. "I don't suppose you have an extra one in your pack?"

"No, I'm afraid not," Badger replied, "but who are you? I'm Badger and this is my best friend, Fox."

"Pleased to meet you, Badger and Fox," the rat said brightly. "I'm Rat, but my friends call me Packer."

"Hi, Packer," Fox nodded. "Do you live in this cave?"

"Yes," said Packer. "I decided it was a good place to build a house 'cause it wouldn't get wet." Then he added, "Would you like to see it? It's right over there."

After a few steps, Packer stopped. "There it is," he said proudly and pointed to a jumble of sticks and mud and who knows what built into a hollow on one side of the cave. "I'm sorry I can't ask you in, but I'm making improvements at the moment."

"That's a fine house," Badger remarked politely, happy they couldn't go in. Fox nodded but said nothing.

"Where do *you* live?" Packer asked.

"Far, far away," Fox answered, waving towards the cave's entrance, "all the way up to the top of the hill and down the other side and across a river…I'm exhausted just thinking about it."

"I can show you a shortcut back through the cave," Packer offered – and then added with a smile, "I'll trade you a shortcut for a shiny button."

Suddenly Fox remembered something. "Well, we don't have another shiny button, but how would you like some shiny paper?" And she pulled from her pocket the crumpled piece of tin foil that had been wrapped around the chocolate bar.

"That's a very nice piece of shiny paper," Packer said approvingly. Then he added, "And it smells delicious!"

So Packer agreed to show Badger and Fox the shortcut back through the cave. "You're sure it's safe?" Badger asked. "How will we see in the dark?"

"Oh, don't worry a bit," Packer reassured her. "I've taken this shortcut so many times, I'd know my way blindfolded. You just hold on tight to Fox's tail and Fox will hold on to my tail, and we'll be all set."

Packer's self-confidence was convincing, but as the three set off and the light from the cave's entrance grew smaller and smaller, Badger and Fox both began to get nervous. Then suddenly the tunnel took a sharp turn, and it was completely dark – darker than the forest on a moonless night, darker than a closet with the door closed, darker than being in bed with eyes shut tight under all the covers. Badger tightened her grip on Fox's tail and Fox, her grip on Packer's.

Suddenly Badger thought she felt something brush against her face. "Eek," she cried and shook her head, "what was that?"

"Probably just some falling dirt," Packer suggested.

"Uh oh," Fox warned, "I hear water running."

"Not to worry," Packer insisted. "There are lots of underground streams, but they don't cross this tunnel."

Then the stillness became as deep as the darkness.

Down, down, down they stumbled and staggered and slipped, following the tunnel now to the left, now to the right, now slightly up, now steeply down. "Packer," Badger asked softly, "are you sure this is the way?"

"Packer," Fox whispered, "this is a very long shortcut."

But Packer's voice remained completely calm: "Just a little farther. – Don't worry." At last, far up ahead, they saw a small circle of daylight. "Hooray!" Fox shouted.

"Three cheers for Packer," Badger cried.

✳

Coming out into the light and looking around, they saw they were indeed back at the river. The sun on their faces felt delicious. Fox did a little dance. "So you like my shortcut?" Packer asked with a big smile. "I know lots of shortcuts. Next time you visit, I'll show you another one."

"And," said Badger, "next time we visit, we'll bring you a shiny button!"

The Mysterious Visitor

One evening after supper Badger was sitting in a comfy chair reading while Fox sat on her bed strumming her guitar. Badger was so absorbed in her book, she didn't even hear Fox playing, and Fox was so absorbed in her playing she didn't even see the excitement on Badger's face. Finally, after a while, Badger put down her book and looked up. "Fox," she said with a smile, "this is such a good mystery story. Why don't *we* have good mysteries to solve? Don't you think that would be fun?"

"Maybe," said Fox, "but I've already got lots of mysteries to solve. Just today I discovered one of my striped socks had disappeared into thin air. I've looked for it everywhere, but it's simply disappeared. That's a pretty good mystery if you ask me." And with that Fox stopped strumming her guitar and poked around in the piles of clothing she always left on the floor. "It just disappeared," she said again.

"I was actually thinking of a different kind of mystery," Badger continued, "more like finding a missing treasure or getting a visit from a mysterious stranger. – You know, something really, really tricky to figure out."

"But that's the problem with my sock!" Fox persisted. "It's really, really tricky to figure out what happened to it," and she poked again at the clothing on the floor.

Badger put down her book and walked over to Fox's bed. For a few minutes she stood there looking around. "Do you remember when you last saw your sock?" Badger asked.

"I think I had it last Tuesday or Wednesday, the day it rained so hard," Fox said a little uncertainly. Badger walked over to her friend's rain boots which were still standing in a corner by the door. She looked at both of them, reached into one, and pulled out a striped sock.

*

"Wow!" Fox shouted, "You're one good detective! I also lost a lot of other things. Can you help me find them too?"

"Sure," said Badger, "just make a list and we can look for them tomorrow. But before Fox could make her list, she found something else she wanted to do and forgot about the list completely. Meanwhile Badger went back to her book – but not for long.

The den was now perfectly quiet. Suddenly Badger stopped reading. She had a puzzled look on her face. Somewhere nearby she could hear faint scratching sounds. She tried to ignore them but couldn't. "Fox," she finally asked, "do you hear something?"

Fox listened for a few seconds. "I think I hear some leaves or maybe a branch scratching against the door. Is it windy?" Badger got up to look. No, it wasn't windy, and there was nothing rubbing against the door.

The two friends again listened carefully. The sounds seemed to be getting louder. "Where's that coming from?" Badger asked.

"I can't tell," Fox said, "but somewhere close by," and she poked again at the clothing scattered around her bed. Suddenly, a T-shirt moved by itself. "Look!" Fox pointed as a corner of the shirt began to rise up off the floor – Badger was too astonished to say a word.

*

Higher and higher the T-shirt rose as if by magic. There were no more scratching sounds, but a muffled huffing and puffing and wheezing had taken their place. Finally, the T-shirt slid off to one side, and standing in front of the two friends was the strangest animal they had ever seen! It was about the size of a chipmunk. It had no visible ears, tiny, almost invisible eyes, and big, scaly paws. It also had what looked like a bright pink flower on the tip of its nose!

✳

For several minutes Badger and Fox just stared at the mysterious visitor. At last the newcomer reached into a pocket and took out a pair of very thick glasses. Carefully she balanced them on her long snout.

"Ah, that's a little better," she smiled – then added, "I'm not used to such a bright moon. – Rather odd, don't you think, I mean, on such a cloudy night?" She looked up towards the ceiling where a little light was hanging. Badger and Fox traded puzzled looks. Neither was sure what the newcomer meant.

"Hi, I'm Badger" said Badger, smiling a bit nervously.

"And I'm Fox," said Fox, "and that's my T-shirt." She pointed to the T-shirt lying next to the hole in the floor.

"Ah, yes, very attractive," the newcomer said, still staring at the ceiling.

"And what's your name?" Badger asked.

"Oh, right, my name is Star," the visitor replied.

"Pleased to meet you, Star," said Badger, and when Star continued to stare at the ceiling as though it were the most interesting thing around, Badger added, "Is there perhaps something we can do for you?" By this point Fox was also staring at the ceiling trying to figure out what Star found so interesting. "Excuse me," Badger asked again in a somewhat louder voice, "but I'm wondering whether you need some help."

"Could be," Star finally replied, looking vaguely in Badger's direction, "but I was so sure I knew where I was."

At this point the pedals of the pink flower at the tip of Star's nose began to wiggle and wriggle and quiver and writhe faster and faster. Fox found this so fascinating, her own whiskers began to twitch as if in sympathy.

"A worm," Star suddenly murmured. "Somewhere nearby I feel a worm – a fat, juicy worm, a sweet, savory worm, the kind of worm my heart yearns for and my stomach churns for." With a big sigh she turned and approached a coat rack where several sweaters and a hat were hanging. "Do you perhaps, friend Badger, have a worm you can spare a hungry traveler?" She smiled and brought her paws together explaining, "I'm afraid I missed my supper."

Badger looked at Fox and Fox at Badger while Star continued to smile at the coat rack. "I'm afraid we have no worms," Badger apologized.

"You know," Fox added, "I can't even remember when we last had any – for supper, I mean."

There was a long silence. Then Badger suggested, "Why don't you look in our fridge and see if there's something else you might like."

"Your fridge?" Star asked. "There's a fridge out here? Where is it?"

*

"It's this way," Badger motioned, gently taking Star's arm and leading her to the refrigerator. But no sooner had Badger opened the refrigerator door than the pedals of the pink flower at the tip of Star's nose began again to wiggle and wriggle and quiver and writhe, if anything, even faster than before. Then – zip, zip, zip, zip, zip – more quickly than either Badger or Fox could follow – a whole plate of sardines simply disappeared. Star looked up happily, one fish tail still sticking out of a corner of her mouth.

"How did you do that?" Fox asked in amazement. "I mean, that was incredible. One second there was a plate of sardines and the next there was only a plate! Are you a magician or something?"

"Please, please," Star replied. "You praise me too much."

"Do you think you could teach me that trick?" Fox persisted.

"Perhaps another time when it's not so late," Star answered. "Right now I can see by the moon I should be going." Fox looked at the ceiling and shrugged.

"Are you sure you don't want something else?" Badger asked.

"No, no," Star reassured her. "You've been very kind. Now if you could just show me to my hole."

So Badger again took Star by the arm and led her back to the hole in the floor. Star took off her glasses and put them back in a pocket. Then she waved vaguely in Badger and Fox's direction and disappeared.

"Well," said Fox after a long silence, "you wanted a good mystery, and now we've had one. "What kind of animal was that?"

"I'm not sure," Badger frowned thoughtfully. "Let's see: We know she spends lots of time digging tunnels and looking for worms to eat – that's why she doesn't see well but has those big, scaly paws."

"So far," replied Fox, "that sounds like a mole – but what about the flower on the end of her nose? And the way she made those sardines vanish like…" Fox snapped her fingers. "I've never seen a mole like that!"

"Me either," Badger agreed. "Let's take a look in my *Animal Encyclopedia*," and see what we find. Quickly Badger found her book and opened it to the section on moles. "Hey, Fox, look at this picture," she cried and held up the open book.

"It's Star!" Fox agreed. "What does it say?"

Badger read: "The *Star-Nosed Mole* is named for 22 feelers arranged in the form of a star on the end of its nose. Thanks to these feelers it can find and eat food items faster than any other animal on earth."

"So," said Fox, "what I thought was a flower were really those special feelers which also look like a star, and that explains her name."

"Exactly!" Badger nodded, closing the book.

Fox looked at Badger with a big smile on her face. "Badger," she said, "you really are a good detective. I'm so glad you're going to help me find all the things I've lost." And with that the two friends put on their PJs, brushed their teeth, and went to bed.

The Birthday Surprise

One day Badger turned the page of the calendar hanging in the den. "Say, Fox," she called, "do you know whose birthday is coming up?"

"Mine?" Fox guessed.

"No," Badger answered, "Try again!"

"Yours?" Fox guessed.

"No. Try again."

"I give up," Fox said after puzzling a second. "Tell me."

"Rabbit's," Badger announced. "It's Rabbit's birthday next week!"

❋

"I'm so glad I noticed," Badger continued, a serious look on her face. "We need to make him a present."

"What are we going to make him?" Fox asked – then added, "I bet he'd like a chocolate cake. I heard rabbits really like chocolate."

"Everyone likes chocolate," Badger agreed. "But I'd like us to make him something he wouldn't expect. Rabbit loves surprises."

❀

Then, after a little pause, Badger said almost to herself, "Something he likes but wouldn't expect... Too bad it's too early for raspberries. Rabbit really likes raspberries, and we could..."

"Hey," Fox interrupted, "how about strawberries? Yesterday I found a patch that's just about ripe. I could hardly believe it – strawberries this early in the year! Wouldn't Rabbit be surprised by a strawberry shortcake?"

❀

"That's perfect," Badger cried, "absolutely perfect! We can put candles on the cake and sing happy birthday and...and...Hey! Why don't we also give him a party to go with his cake! Wouldn't that be special plus?!"

"A party!" Fox said jumping up in excitement. "We can eat cake and play games and sing songs and have a great time."

"Fox," Badger smiled, "I think we've got a plan."

❀

Badger now had something to organize and that made her very happy. "Okay," she said, grabbing a pencil and a sheet of paper. "You get the strawberries and make up the games, and I'll make the cake and get the candles. Together we'll make a list of Rabbit's friends, write out the invitations, and deliver them. – But," and here Badger sounded a bit worried, "we have to be careful not to let Rabbit know, or it won't be a surprise. Can you keep the party a secret from him?"

"Sure," Fox nodded, "just remind me from time to time."

❊

The first time Fox needed reminding was that very afternoon when Rabbit stopped by for a visit. "Say, Rabbit," Badger asked, trying to sound casual, "any chance you'll be around next Saturday afternoon?"

"Saturday afternoon?" Rabbit thought a moment. "I think so – Why?"

"No reason," Fox answered, "just in case we want to have a part…"

Badger interrupted, "Just in case we want to have a part of the day for…for a little picnic." Badger secretly looked at Fox and made a big silent "NO!" with her lips. Rabbit didn't notice.

❊

Two days later Badger and Fox met Rabbit while taking a walk.

"Hi, Rabbit," they called. "What's up?"

"I'm looking for strawberries," Rabbit answered. "Someone told me they found some already ripe, and I really love strawberries.

Badger and Fox gave each other a knowing little poke.

"Well, good luck," Badger said, thankful that Fox had already picked the berries. "And don't forget Saturday."

❈

"Saturday – what's Saturday?" Rabbit asked, searching behind a bush.

"You know," Fox answered, "your party at our house."

Rabbit looked up startled, "What did you say?"

But before Fox could say another word Badger jumped in. "I agree with Fox – Rabbit, you're hearty as our mouse"

"Hearty as your mouse?" Rabbit stood up, now completely confused. "What does that mean?"

"Oh," Badger explained, "didn't we tell you? We have a mouse visiting us, and it's always so cheerful and lively…so, so hearty."

❃

At this point both Badger and Fox thought the best thing to do was to move on as quickly as possible. "So long, Rabbit," they called. "See you at the picnic on Saturday afternoon," Badger added.

"Whew!" Fox took a deep breath after they had walked a while. "That was close."

Badger shook her head, "It really was. I think you'd better stay away from Rabbit until his birthday. Secrets seem to pop out of your mouth."

"You're right," Fox agreed. "I wonder when I told him about the strawberries."

❃

So Fox stayed away from Rabbit and instead worked on ways to make the party fun. She put jelly beans in little bags and hid them around the den (even under her pillow). She collected all the musical instruments she and Badger had –drums, rattles, two kazoos, a rain stick, several horns, and, of course, her guitar – and cleared a dance space. She made a tent out of a big blanket and turned a little table into a stage for their puppets. Finally, she filled a paper bag with treats and hung it from the ceiling. They would take turns trying to find it blindfolded.

❁

Meanwhile, Badger wrote out invitations to all of Rabbit's friends. She also made cookies and a big fruit salad as well as a strawberry shortcake. Then, after the two of them had cleaned up the clothing Fox always left scattered around her bed, they filled the den with colorful balloons and hung decorations from the walls and ceiling. By the time they finished, they didn't recognize their den, it was so special.

❁

Soon it was the morning of Rabbit's surprise party. Sometime after breakfast, Badger opened the door to see what the weather was like. It was a beautiful spring day, but just as she thought to herself, "what a great day for a party," she saw a folded piece of paper on the ground. "Now what can that be?" she asked, bending to pick it up. "Oh, no," she cried as she read it. "Fox, Fox," she called in alarm. "Look what I just found outside our door."

❁

Fox came running and Badger handed her the note. It was from Rabbit and it read: "Hi, Guys, sorry to change plans at the last minute, but do you mind if we have our picnic tomorrow instead of today? I'm feeling a little sad and want to take a long walk and look again for that special strawberry patch. I'm sure I'll be feeling better tomorrow. Your friend, Rabbit."

"Yikes," Fox cried. "What are we going to do now? He may already have gone off somewhere."

❀

"Let's hope not," Badger said. "Listen, here's what we do. You run off and find him. Tell him you think you know where the strawberry patch is. Then lead him to another part of the forest, stopping at several places to look for it. Just keep him busy until noon. I'll stay here and take care of a few last things before the guests arrive. When it's noon, you can say you suddenly remember exactly where you saw the patch" – she gave Fox a big smile – "and you can lead him right back here!"

❀

"Good plan," said Fox eager to hurry off. "I'm really, really good at finding distractions and wasting time. This will be fun."

"Okay," Badger nodded. "Just remember to come back at noon – and remember to keep the party a secret – just a little bit longer! I'm guessing from Rabbit's note he thinks no one has remembered his special day."

"Don't worry!" Fox reassured her, "I'll be careful," and off she ran.

❀

Fox got to Rabbit's burrow in record time, but when she knocked, no one came to the door. Then through the trees she saw Rabbit not too far away. "Hi, Rabbit," she called after him.

"Oh, hi, Fox," Rabbit said a little sadly. "Did you get my note?"

"We did," Fox replied, "and you know, I think I may have also seen those strawberries, so I came to help you look."

"Great," said Rabbit, brightening up a little.

❀

Then Fox took Rabbit on a very long walk through the forest. Again and again she said she thought the strawberries were here or there or maybe over there – and each time they weren't. When it was almost noon, Rabbit suggested they just give up. "Maybe somebody already picked them," he said.

"Wait, wait," Fox cried one more time. "Yes, yes! How could I have forgotten? Now I remember exactly where I saw them. C'mon, we'll be eating them in no time!"

❀

Off they ran with Fox leading the way back to Badger and Fox's den. When they got there, Rabbit suddenly stopped and looked around in confusion. "But – but this is where you live," he said. "Do you mean this is where the strawberries are?" And just at that moment Badger opened the door and stepped out, holding in her

paws an enormous strawberry shortcake with seven candles on top. Then all Rabbit's friends rushed out behind Badger shouting, "Surprise! Surprise! Happy Birthday, Rabbit!" And Rabbit was indeed surprised – surprised and very, very happy.

The Unusual Present

Badger and Fox were just coming home after a long morning walk. "Look!" said Fox, pointing in the direction of their den, "There's a package in front of our door." And sure enough, right in front of their door lay a big box wrapped in sturdy brown paper.

"Let's see what it is," Badger cried, and with that the two friends ran to find out.

❁

"It's from my Great Aunt Badger," Badger announced, reading the return address.

"I wonder what she sent you," Fox asked. "Maybe it's something fun!"

"What she sent *us*," Badger corrected her friend. "Look at the address."

"Ms. Badger and Ms. Fox," Fox read. "Yippee! She sent me a present too! I can't believe it. C'mon, let's open it." So they quickly carried it inside.

Grip – Rip – Claw – Gnaw – Pull, Shred, Tear! Before they knew it, the brown wrapping paper lay in pieces all around them. Badger folded back the top flaps of the box. It was filled to the brim with fluffy white tissue paper. "Wow! That's a lot of paper," Fox said, shaking her head. Badger began removing it, piece by piece, but it seemed to have no end. "Maybe that's all she sent us," Badger suggested. "My great aunt always did have a strange sense of humor."

❋

Finally, they saw something pink – a pink ribbon that was attached to something else. "What is it?" Fox asked, leaning forward to get a better look. Carefully Badger lifted it out. The ribbon was fastened to a dress – the frilliest, laciest, fanciest dress either of them had ever seen. It was all white except for a band of strawberries sewn on both the collar and the little puff

sleeves. Around the waist ran the pink ribbon.

Badger and Fox stared at it speechless. Then Badger removed some more tissue paper and lifted out a second dress, just like the first except that sewn around the collar and the sleeves were raspberries, and the ribbon around the waist was lavender. Badger held up the second dress. Well, Fox," she said at last, "it was very kind of my great aunt to send one to each of us."

❋

Badger laid the dresses on her bed side by side. "They look a little like cotton candy," she suggested.

"Too bad we can't eat them!" Fox remarked.

"But what *can* we do with them?" Badger asked, turning to Fox. "When would we ever wear them?"

"You're asking me?" Fox shook her head. "I wear only sweats and T-shirts."

❋

"Well," said Badger with a sigh, "the least we can do is try them on. Maybe something will occur to us. – So, Fox, which one do you want?"

Fox made a funny face and then announced: "I'm more the raspberry type." Badger handed her the second dress. Then Badger slipped off her jeans and tried on her new dress. She glanced in a mirror and broke out laughing. Then she glanced at Fox and started howling. – Fox had put her dress on *over* her sweats.

"I think," Fox said, "I'm going to twirl" – and suddenly she started dancing all over the den, twirling and whirling and making her skirt fly out.

"Me too!" Badger shouted, and she too began twirling and whirling and skipping and dipping."

"La, la, la," they sang, "tra, la, la," and they kept twirling and whirling until finally they crashed into each other and collapsed on Badger's bed.

❁

"That was fun," Badger said, panting and trying to catch her breath. "I really do like to twirl. What else can we do with these dresses?" There was a long silence.

Finally Fox suggested, "Hey, let's go ask some of our friends. Maybe one of them will have an idea."

"Do you think so?" Badger asked.

"There's only one way to find out," Fox replied. And without another word, they set off to ask their friends."

❁

The first friend they ran into was Raccoon. She was crouching at the side of a pond, looking for fish. "Hi, Raccoon," Badger called out.

Raccoon looked over her shoulder and almost tumbled into the water in surprise. "Badger, Fox – is that really

you?!! – You look like you're up to something…
something special."

"We are," answered Fox, who made a little curtsy.

"We just got these dresses from my great aunt,"
Badger explained, and we're not sure what to do with
them. – Any ideas?"

❋

"Oh," Raccoon replied, relieved that Badger and Fox
were as puzzled as she was. "Well, maybe…if I had
gotten a dress like that…maybe…Oh, yes, I know! If
I had gotten a dress like that, I would use it as a fish
net! I would stand in the water and hold out the sides
and wait for a fish to get tangled in it. Want to give it a
try?" Fox looked at Badger, who looked unconvinced.

"Maybe later," Badger said. "For now we're just
collecting ideas." – And off they went.

❋

The next friend they met was Squirrel, who was
sitting on a tree branch eating an acorn. When she saw
Badger and Fox, at first she didn't recognize them and
got ready to scamper up the tree.

"Hi, Squirrel," Badger called, "you look upset. Are
you okay?" Now Squirrel recognized them, and the
acorn fell out of her mouth.

"Um, um, I…" Squirrel stammered. "You look…You
look…different."

"It's our dresses," Fox explained. "They're a present from Badger's great aunt, and we don't know what they're good for. Got any ideas?"

❀

Squirrel studied the dresses carefully for several long minutes. "I got it," she finally announced. "They'd make great parachutes. You could jump from a high branch holding out the skirt, and you'd float to the ground like a leaf. Want to try?" Although Fox was interested, Badger had her doubts. "I'll definitely put that on our list," she assured Squirrel, "but for now we're only gathering suggestions." – And off they went again.

❀

The next friend they met was Rabbit who was hunting for early raspberries. "Wow!" he said when he saw them, his face breaking into a big grin, "where are you going dressed like that?"

"We're coming to see you," Badger replied. "We just got these dresses from my Great Aunt Badger, and we're not sure what to do with them. What do you think?"

❀

Rabbit wriggled his way free from the bush he was in. "I see you've got berries of your own," he laughed, pointing to the bands of strawberries and raspberries on the two dresses. "Maybe those are berry-picking dresses – but, no, I don't think so. They'd get caught on the thorns in a minute….hmm....hmm." He scratched his right ear with his left ear. Then he said, "You need to ask someone who already has such a dress….Let's see…Skunk! Skunk has one! She got it last year!"

❀

"I knew Rabbit would be able to help," Badger smiled as she and Fox made their way to Skunk's den.

"Let's hope Skunk can also help," Fox added. Soon they were knocking on Skunk's door.

"Oh, what a lovely surprise!" Skunk beamed, opening her door. "I must have forgotten you were coming. Please wait just a minute. I'll be right back." And a minute later she reappeared wearing the same kind of dress Badger and Fox were wearing.

❀

"Come in, oh, do come in," she insisted. "My, you do look lovely. Those dresses are so attractive."As a matter of fact, she wasn't sure what to make of Fox's outfit, but she smiled nonetheless.

"And you look lovely too," Badger replied.

"Yes, very nice," Fox agreed.

"Well, thank you so much. Now please sit down while I get us some lemonade, and then we can chat." So Badger and Fox each sat down in a comfy chair and waited while Skunk got some lemonade.

❊

"So nice of you to visit," she began again, and in such beautiful dresses."

"Actually," said Badger, "we just got them today from my great aunt."

"Well, she certainly does have good taste," Skunk nodded approvingly.

"But maybe you can answer a question," Fox said slowly.

Skunk looked at Fox and smiled, "Yes?"

"We don't know exactly what these dresses are for – and we thought maybe you could tell us since you already have one."

❊

"Oh, that's easy," Skunk replied. "They're for saying nice things about."

There was a long silence. Then Fox asked, "That's it?"

"That's a lot," Skunk assured her. "Saying nice things is very, very important." Then she added, "I love the way your ribbon matches your, uh, pants."

Fox and Badger both looked at Fox's sweats and noticed for the first time they were also a kind of lavender – just like her ribbon.

❀

"You're right," Badger agreed, "saying nice things *is* important, and sometimes it's good to be reminded." Then she added brightly, "I really like the yellow butterflies on your dress." There was a silence. She caught Fox's eye.

"Yes," Fox nodded, "very nice butterflies, and they match your lemonade."

There was another silence while they finished their drinks.

❀

"What an interesting visit!" Badger said as she and Fox returned to their den. "I think I really did learn something – and not just what these dresses are good for."

"I guess so," Fox agreed, "but, to tell the truth, I can't wait to take mine off and go raspberry hunting."

"I think I'll keep mine on a while and do some more twirling," Badger announced. Then she shouted, "Last one home is a lemon!"

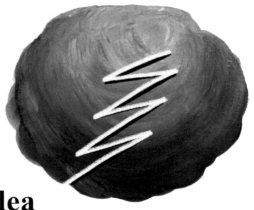

The Great Idea

"Badger, Badger," Fox shouted as she tumbled into their den. Badger looked up from the picture she was drawing. Fox grabbed her guitar and leapt up onto her bed.

"What is it, Fox?" Badger asked as Fox started to sing.

"Badger," Fox cried, leaping off her bed and rushing over to where Badger was sitting. "Badger, I just had a great idea!"

✳

"Fantastic," said Badger with a big smile. "What is it?"

"Well," said Fox, "you know how much I love to sing and play my guitar."

"I do," said Badger, nodding at the guitar Fox was still holding. "And," Fox continued, putting the guitar down on Badger's drawing, "you know how much I also love to dance and do all kinds of jazzy moves." And before Badger could say another word, Fox knocked over a floor lamp and a chair while doing a jazzy move.

✳

"Not only that," Fox went on, "but I know lots of jokes and stories and riddles."

"Right," said Badger, "so what's your great idea?"

"Can't you tell?" Fox beamed. "We should have a talent show, so all our friends can see my talents."

"You mean a one-animal talent show?" Badger asked slowly.

"Why not?" answered Fox. "I've got lots of talents."

"Because," Badger pointed out, "the whole purpose of a talent show is to give lots of folks a chance to show their talents."

✳

Fox thought for a moment. "I've got it," she announced. "It wouldn't really be a one-animal show because you would be the one who organized it and directed it. You could build the stage and make a list of everyone who wants to come and show them where to sit. We both know you're very, very good at making lists and organizing things."

"Well," said Badger, who did indeed love to make lists and organize things, "let's try a slightly different plan. I could make a list of all the things needed to make a stage and get the stage built, and if we also gave other animals a chance to perform, I could make a list of everyone who wanted to perform and…"

"But I could perform first…" Fox interrupted.

"Why not?" Badger replied. "It's your great idea!"

❊

For the next few days the two friends went happily about their different tasks. Then Rabbit stopped by for a visit. "Hi, Badger," Rabbit said, "What are you up to?"

"I'm making a list of all the animals I should tell about Fox's great idea."

"What's Fox's great idea?" Rabbit asked.

"To have a show where everyone can share their talents."

Badger didn't mention that Fox had only talked about her own talents.

❊

"Wow!" Rabbit gave a delighted chuckle. "That *is* a great idea. I could do a magic trick I learned from my uncle. But," Rabbit continued, looking around, "where would we perform?"

"Well," Badger said, "we would need to build a stage somewhere in the forest."

"That's also a great idea," Rabbit nodded, and Badger was very pleased he thought so.

Badger then showed Rabbit her list of all the things they would need to build a stage. "I've also made a list of friends who might want to help build it," she said as she pulled out another list. Then she added, blushing a little, "And look, Rabbit, you're at the very top."

"Great!" Rabbit cried, "Let's check out the rest of the list." And without another word, they set out to do so.

❊

Meanwhile, Fox was busy practicing her talents. Mostly she practiced playing the guitar and singing. But on Monday she also practiced dancing and on Tuesday telling stories and on Wednesday doing somersaults and skipping rope. By Saturday she was completely exhausted and slept till noon. On Sunday she said to Badger: "I'm glad my great idea is only a week away. I'm getting really tired getting so good at so many things!"

✳

By the day of the show Badger and Rabbit had everything ready to go. Together with Beaver and several other friends, they had built a sturdy stage in a grassy clearing. They had also hung streamers from the trees around the clearing and had made a banner that read:

BIG FOREST TALENT SHOW

There was plenty of room for everyone to sit on the ground around the stage or, if they wanted, on branches of the surrounding trees.

Many animals had signed up to perform. Raccoon wanted to show how good she was at opening closed boxes and bins and just about everything else. Owl said he knew a lot of riddles and funny questions beginning with "Whooo?" The Porcupine Twins hoped to have a quill-shooting contest, and Possum said she could play possum for as long as anyone wanted. Squirrel planned to dazzle the audience with acrobatic leaps among the trees, and Rabbit rehearsed the magic trick he had learned from his uncle – complete with an old top hat.

Fox, of course, would be the first to perform, and she was still hoping to show quite a few of her many talents. But Badger, who was announcing the performers, reminded her how important it was that everyone get a turn. At the last minute Rabbit suggested Badger wear his uncle's top hat – when Rabbit wasn't using it – because it would make her look more official. Fox thought the hat made Badger look more funny than official.

※

The morning of the show arrived beautiful and clear – only a few puffy clouds in a bright blue sky. Since the show might last for hours, many animals brought blankets to sit on and food to snack on. By early afternoon everything was ready and everyone was

eager to start. Badger noticed that the sky had gotten a little darker, but after the sun came back, she decided it was only a passing cloud.

Then, just as Badger stepped onto the stage wearing Rabbit's uncle's top hat, the sky again grew darker. "Welcome! Welcome to the Big Forest Talent Show," Badger beamed. Everyone sitting around the stage on the grass and in the trees cheered. Badger was just about to say something else when suddenly they all heard a long roll of thunder – and it did not seem that far away.

"Uh-oh," Badger said to no one in particular.

Fox, however, who was sitting right next to the stage and had overheard her, looked up at the sky and said, "Don't worry. I still see some blue."

"Maybe," Badger answered, "but look over there, and she pointed behind Fox to where the biggest, darkest rain cloud she had ever seen was sliding into view.

Then came another, even scarier rumble of thunder as Fox grabbed her guitar and jumped up onto the stage. Badger now looked very worried but bravely announced, "To begin our show, we have Fox playing her guitar and singing…" A dazzling bolt of lightning flashed across the sky. Everyone looked up and several animals shuddered. Badger was just about to continue when suddenly she realized she had no idea what Fox wanted to sing. "Fox," she whispered, "what are you going to sing?"

✳

Fox herself suddenly looked uncertain. She had practiced so many songs, she had forgotten to pick any favorites. Then, as the first large raindrop splashed on the stage, she made up her mind and out came

> *Oh, it ain't gonna rain no more, no more*
> *It ain't gonna rain no more*
> *How in the heck can I wash my neck*
> *if it ain't gonna rain no more!*

✳

But it did rain some more – and some more – and some more! Soon raindrops were splashing everywhere on the stage and on the grass, making instant puddles. Not only that, but the thunder rolling through the trees was so loud, no one could hear Fox's song. Finally, when a giant lightning bolt hit a tree on the other side of the clearing, Fox stopped. For a few seconds, everything seemed very quiet. The animals all looked at each other nervously, ready to run or fly – at the drop of Badger's top hat.

✳

"Hey, everybody," they suddenly heard Fox shout, "I have a great idea! Let's move our talent show to another day and have a dance party in the deserted barn instead."

"Great idea, great idea!" Badger shouted back, waving a now-very-wet top hat in the direction of the barn. So everyone cheered and off they hopped, scurried, scampered, or flew. Fox, of course, sang many, many songs at the party, and everyone danced till it rained no more.

The Daring Rescue

"It's so hot," Fox moaned. "I wish I didn't have to wear this fur coat. She was sitting under a tree sipping a glass of lemonade. Badger was sitting on the other side of the same tree reading a book.

"Hey, Fox," Badger suddenly said and poked her head around the trunk, "you do have a bathing suit. Why don't you put it on and shuffle over to the river? I heard Otter is giving swimming lessons in the big pool near his den."

✳

"Oh, I don't know," Fox replied. "I'm not really the swimming type."

"But you're also not the 'I'm too hot' type. C'mon. I'll go with you. Even if we don't go swimming, it'll be cooler by the river. We can take a big blanket to lie on and some snacks in case we get hungry."

"This idea is sounding better and better," Fox replied. "Okay!"

So they put on their bathing suits, packed some snacks, found a big blanket to lie on and set off. As it turned out, they were not the only ones going to the river. On their way they met Squirrel who was taking her nephew there. Beechnut was the little squirrel's name and he was very excited. This was his first visit to the forest, and like Squirrel he had more energy than he knew what to do with. Even Squirrel was having a hard time keeping up with him as he scurried up and down the trees along the path.

Before long they could hear lots of splashing and laughing. It was the Porcupine Twins having a water fight in the big pool near Otter's den. Then, as they came closer, they saw Otter himself in the middle of the pool showing Raccoon how he used his tail to get extra speed when swimming. In another part of the pool Rabbit was doing a slow bunny paddle while talking to Turtle who glided along beside him.

❋

"Hi, everyone," the newcomers called. "How's the water?"

"Great!" Otter called back. "Do you want a swimming lesson?"

"Maybe a little later," Badger answered while Beechnut scampered off and Squirrel ran after him.

"Be careful," Squirrel called to her nephew, "and don't fall in the water! – I hope you know how to swim!" Beechnut had raced up a big tree and was now exploring branches that arched out over the river.

✳

Badger unfolded the blanket she and Fox had brought. "I'm already hungry," Fox said as she checked out the snacks. She found two plump peaches and handed one to Badger. After Fox had eaten hers, she announced, "I think I'll do some rock hopping. Want to come?"

"No thanks," Badger replied, "I think I'll just stay around here and wade in the water."

"See you later," Fox called as she made her way towards a steep tumble of rocks where the river fell with a roar into the big pool.

✳

All of a sudden there was a shriek – it was a tiny shriek but it was definitely a shriek.

Then everyone heard Squirrel scream, "Oh, no! …
Beechnut!" At the very end of a branch that reached
out over the waterfall, Beechnut was clinging to a twig
that had broken but still dangled. The little squirrel
and the twig slowly swayed in the spray that rose from
between a pair of enormous boulders.

❋

Fox had just climbed one of those very boulders when
they heard Squirrel scream. In a minute Badger and
all the others were standing beside Fox. Meanwhile,
Squirrel had raced up to the thicker end of the branch
Beechnut was hanging from. Every time the little
squirrel swung in the breeze, she would start to inch
out towards him, only to realize the branch would
never support the two of them. Should it break, she
and Beechnut would both plunge into the churning
water.

❋

Below them, on the big boulder, everyone was trying
to figure out what to do. Someone suggested they run
and try to find Owl who could pluck the little squirrel
up in his talons and carry him to safety. But who knew
where Owl was and how long such a rescue might
take? Otter said he could swim to the base of the
waterfall and wait in case Beechnut should let go or
the twig should snap. But the water beneath the falls
was rough, and Beechnut could be underwater a long
time before Otter found him.

＊

Suddenly Badger grabbed Fox's arm. "Fox," she said, "can you and Rabbit find a way to get across the river quickly?"

Fox looked upstream beyond the waterfall. "Sure," she said and pointed to a place where the river flowed slowly around a little island.

Without another word she and Rabbit raced up to the island and got across. Soon they were racing back down the other side.

✳

Meanwhile, Badger ran to get the blanket she and Fox had brought. "We'll need a long stick, strong enough to hold this blanket," she told the others. One of the Porcupine Twins quickly found exactly what she wanted.

"Okay," she called across to Fox and Rabbit, "Can you come out onto the big boulder opposite the one we're on?" Fox was already on her way. "Careful," Badger warned. "It looks slippery."

✳

It was indeed slippery, and Fox and Rabbit took no chances. Getting down on all four paws, they crept across the boulder. Badger now wrapped the blanket around the long stick, tying it at both ends with a piece of vine. "Okay, everyone," she cried, "Let's try to pass one end of the stick to Fox and Rabbit." Despite the roar of the water, they could still hear Beechnut whimpering above them. "Don't worry, Beechnut," Squirrel called out to him. "You'll be safe in a minute." – At least that's what she hoped.

✳

With Badger, Otter, Raccoon, and the Porcupine Twins all holding it tightly, the stick began to move across the gap between the two boulders. "Don't lean out too far," Badger warned, and everyone made sure they didn't. Carefully Fox grabbed the far end of the stick. "Good work!" Badger shouted. "Now if we can just unroll the blanket without dropping it into the water." Badger and Rabbit each untied the piece of vine at their end.

✳

Finally, everything was ready for the daring rescue. Badger took one corner of the blanket, Otter another, Fox a third, and Rabbit a fourth. Then they spread out the four corners as far as they could. The Porcupine Twins looked on, their eyes wide open. Beneath the terrified little squirrel there now stretched a big safety net. The only question was – would Beechnut use it?

✳

"All set over here," Badger called.

"All set over here," Fox called back.

"Okay, Beechnut," Squirrel said gently, "you can let go now. The blanket will catch you. Just let go and you'll be safe."

But Beechnut was too frightened to let go. Instead he continued to whimper and swing slowly from the half-broken twig. "Please, Beechnut," Squirrel tried again to persuade him. "Just let go and you'll be safe. Just let yourself fall into the blanket."

.

But Beechnut just couldn't, and the rescuers holding the blanket were beginning to get tired. "Well, I'm just going to have to crawl out on that branch until it breaks," Squirrel finally decided. "Okay, Beechnut," she called, "I'm coming to get you." But before she had moved even a tail's length, the twig broke on its own and down fell Beechnut – Plop! – right into the middle of the blanket.

Everyone cheered – everyone except Beechnut who was still too dazed to move and just lay in the blanket blinking. Then, when he realized he really was safe, he dashed to the corner Badger was holding and leapt up onto Badger's head. Again everyone cheered – and forgot to keep a firm hold on the blanket which plunged into the rushing river and disappeared. Minutes later it floated to the surface in the middle of the pool.

The crisis was over. Squirrel took Beechnut home and promised him a big bowl of his favorite treat – beechnuts. Badger and Fox spread their blanket to dry in the sun, and everyone else went back to swimming. Even Badger and Fox decided to swim a little.

"Well, Fox," Badger said as the two paddled slowly side by side, "aren't you glad we didn't just stay home and complain about the heat?"

"Badger," Fox said, "you are one cool critter," and she laughed as she splashed her friend with her tail.

The Special Password

"Badger! Fox! Badger! Fox!" Rabbit shouted as he ran down the path to their den. Badger and Fox were outside in their garden. "You'll never guess what Woodchuck just found!" Whatever it was, they could tell by the big smile on Rabbit's face that it must be something good.

"What is it? What is it?" they asked.

"Well," said Rabbit lowering his voice to a whisper, "he just found an empty den. It's big and comfy and," Rabbit nodded, "very special."

"Wow," said Fox, with a laugh, "where is it?"

"I can't say exactly," Rabbit replied, but it's near the hill with all the birch trees. He said the entrance is hidden by boulders."

"Maybe it was a bear's den," Badger guessed. "I heard there once was a bear that lived in this forest. What does Woodchuck want to use it for?"

"I bet it would make a great clubhouse," Fox suggested.

"Fox!" Rabbit shouted, "That's *exactly* what Woodchuck said!"

❁

Later that same afternoon, Badger, Fox, and Rabbit met Woodchuck to explore the new den. The entrance was so well hidden, it took Woodchuck some time to find it. "It's very dark inside," Woodchuck warned, "but I have a candle."

"And I brought two flashlights," added Badger as she fished them out of her backpack. She and Rabbit shared one flashlight, and Fox and Woodchuck the other. Woodchuck led the way past several big boulders, down a little slope, and around some more boulders.

❁

"How did you ever find this?" Rabbit asked.

"Just luck," Woodchuck answered. "I was looking for a place to nap."

Beyond the entrance the den opened out – both on the sides and overhead. As the four friends explored the walls and ceiling with their flashlights, they could not believe what they saw.

"It's so clean and dry," Badger wondered.

"It's amazing," Rabbit agreed.

"Can we make it a clubhouse?" Fox asked.

"Not just a clubhouse," Woodchuck smiled, "a very special clubhouse. You know, the kind you get invited to join."

"Who would do the inviting," Badger asked, suddenly a little uneasy.

"We would," Woodchuck said, smiling again. – "I thought we could call it 'The Den Club' because so many of our friends live in dens."

"But," Fox pointed out, "we also have friends who don't live in dens."

"Yeah," said Rabbit, "like me – I live in a burrow. Or Beaver. He lives in a lodge."

"No problem," Woodchuck replied. "A burrow or a lodge is just another kind of den anyway."

"But what about Squirrel?" Fox asked. "She lives in a hollow tree." "Or Owl?" Badger added. "He also lives in a tree."

Woodchuck now looked puzzled. "Hmm, I hadn't thought about that. We certainly would want Squirrel and Owl to join." Finally he frowned, "But somehow we need to make our club special."

"I know," Rabbit cried. "We can have a special password you need to get in."

"And it won't matter where someone lives!" Badger added brightly.

"Suppose I forget the password?" Fox asked.

"Don't worry," Rabbit smiled. "If you forget, we'll just remind you!"

Everyone agreed this was a good way to have a special club, and Rabbit suggested that the special password be *Friends.* Everyone thought *Friends* was perfect. They then decided they should have a few club rules. Badger suggested everyone should take a turn bringing a favorite game, and Fox suggested everyone should take a turn bringing a favorite song, and Rabbit suggested everyone should take a turn bringing a favorite snack. Again everyone agreed, and the club now had three rules.

Finally, they decided they should meet again next week and use the time till then letting others know about the club and what you needed to do to get in. "Make sure you tell them," Woodchuck insisted, "if you want to get in, you have to know the special password: *Friends.*" He even made a sign for the club's entrance. The sign read:

SPECIAL CLUBHOUSE

SPECIAL PASSWORD NEEDED

On the day of the first meeting, Woodchuck brought with him a large lantern. Badger brought one of her favorite board games: Tangles and Tunnels; Fox brought a song and her guitar, and Rabbit a basket of apples. However, by the time the meeting was supposed to start, only Bat and the Porcupine Twins had joined them. After a while Skunk also came but had to be reminded what the password was. They all sat in a circle around the lantern except for Bat who preferred to hang from the ceiling in one of the dark corners.

"I wonder where everyone is?" Woodchuck finally asked. "Badger, did you talk to Squirrel?"

"I did," Badger answered, "but she doesn't like being underground too much. Owl told me he doesn't like being underground either."

"I met Beaver and Turtle by the pond this morning," Fox reported, "but they said they were very busy right now. Maybe they'd join later."

"And Possum sleeps all day," Rabbit noted and then added, "Maybe Raccoon forgot."

"Well," Woodchuck sighed, digging at the ground with a stick, "it seemed like such a good idea." And just at that moment they heard a rustling sound at the entrance. "Here comes someone," Rabbit said, and Woodchuck immediately cheered up. "I bet it's Raccoon – or maybe Beaver or Squirrel or Turtle changed their mind. I bet… " but before Woodchuck could finish, out of the darkness slid a large red and yellow snake!

"Hi, Snake," Fox called out.

"Hi, Guys," Snake answered, slithering up to the edge of the circle, his tongue flicking in and out. "Sorry I'm late. I had trouble finding this place. Turtle's directions were a little confusing." Snake raised his head, turned to the left, to the right, and looked up at the ceiling. "A very nice den indeed," he nodded. "In my opinion, the perfect place for a special club."

❁

By now Woodchuck had recovered from his surprise. "Yes," he said, "yes, indeed, a *special* club. I hope you know the special password."

Snake looked puzzled. "Special password?" he asked. "Turtle didn't say anything about a special password."

"Oh, too bad," Woodchuck shook his head. "You need to know the special password to get in. That's what makes this club special."

❁

"Don't worry, Snake," Fox spoke up. "I can tell you the password."

"No, you can't," Woodchuck interrupted, again shaking his head. "Someone already needs to know the password to get in."

"But Skunk didn't know it when she came, and we reminded her what it is," Fox objected.

"Well," said Woodchuck. "That's because she forgot it. She still knew it somewhere, and we just helped her find it."

❁

"That's not much of a difference," Badger pointed out. "Suppose Snake and I go outside, and I tell him the password there?"

"Oh, let's just tell him!" Rabbit said, and everyone except Woodchuck nodded in agreement. He was again digging at the ground.

"Woodchuck," Badger said looking at him kindly. "Do *you* remember our password?"

"Of course!" Woodchuck cried.

"Whisper it to me," Badger smiled. She went over to Woodchuck and put an arm around his shoulder.

Woodchuck stopped digging and whispered in Badger's ear: "*Friends.*"

"Do you really mean it?" Badger whispered back. "Do you mean it or are you just saying it?"

But before Woodchuck could answer, Fox began singing softly,

> *The more we get together, together, together,*
> *The more we get together, the happier we'll be.*
> *'Cause your friends are my friends and my*
> *friends are your friends.*
> *The more we get together the happier we'll be.*

Then, one by one, the other animals also started singing – even Bat hanging in her dark corner. The singing made Fox want to dance, and so she started rocking gently from side to side. In a flash the other animals were all rocking with her. "Isn't this a great special club?" Fox called out.

"Yes, yes, yes!" everyone cheered. "Three cheers for our special club!"

❁

Woodchuck looked around and saw all the others smiling at him. A big smile spread across his own face. Then he too started singing and rocking and... suddenly he shouted in a happy voice, "Hey, guys, what's our special password?"

And all the others shouted, "*Friends*! Our special password is *Friends*." Snake's eyes sparkled. Then he too shouted happily: "*Friends*, our special password is *Friends*!"

The Prize Pumpkin

"Hey, Badger," Fox asked, jumping into the pile of leaves they had made. "What are you going to wear to Raccoon's pumpkin party?"

"I think I'll go as a clown," Badger replied. "Clowns have lots of fun. – What about you?"

"I think I'll go as Wonder Fox this year."

"I think you went as Wonder Fox last year," Badger recalled.

No, I didn't," Fox shook her head, "Last year I went as Super Fox."

Badger looked puzzled. "Wonder Fox, Super Fox – What's the difference?"

"Big difference," Fox assured her, jumping again into the pile of leaves. "Wonder Fox can make herself invisible but Super Fox can't."

"That is a big difference," Badger agreed.

"Besides," Fox continued, "Wonder Fox knows a way to make people share their chocolate."

"C'mon, Fox. You're just making that up because you want me to share my chocolate with you."

"Oh, no," said Fox. "I want everyone to share their chocolate with me!"

Badger and Fox each took another turn jumping into the leaves. Then Fox asked, "So when are we going to carve our pumpkin? I really want to get started."

"What's your hurry?" Badger asked.

"Well," Fox explained, "this year we have to make it unique, so we can win the prize Raccoon is giving for the best scary pumpkin."

"The best scary pumpkin..." Badger repeated to herself.

Then something very strange happened. – A tall flower nearby began to sway back and forth, sometimes slowly, sometimes quickly. Fox noticed it first and said to Badger, "Hey, look at that flower. It's moving back and forth, but there's no breeze!"

Badger turned to look. "You're right," she said. "That's spooky!"

Then, just as she said that, the flower moved again, and this time its movements were accompanied by a little cry – as if it were in pain – eeee! eeee! eeee!

"THAT really is spooky!" Fox whispered. "What should we do?" Badger was just about to suggest something when – from behind the flower popped Mouse. "Boo!" she said.

"Mouse!" Badger and Fox cried out at the same time.

"I hope I didn't scare you too much," she apologized. "I was walking by and heard you talking about something scary, so I thought I'd play a little trick on you. I hope it wasn't too scary."

"It was scary, Badger nodded, "but it was also a very clever trick."

"Exactly!" Fox agreed. "Really, really clever and just right scary."

"So what's the scary thing you two were talking about?" Mouse asked.

"Well," said Badger, "this year Raccoon is giving a prize to whoever brings the best scary pumpkin to her pumpkin party."

"And we need to figure out how to make our pumpkin unique," Fox added.

"By the way, Mouse," Badger asked, "what are you going to wear to the party?"

"Oh, I'm not going," she said with a little shrug. "I mean what can a mouse go as? I'm so small I wouldn't be much of a hero or a monster or anything else. Everyone would just laugh."

"No they wouldn't," Badger shook her head. "It doesn't make any difference how big you are. You just have to decide what you'd like to be. We could even help you make your costume."

"Sure," Fox nodded, "and costumes are fun to make. You can be anything you want with a good costume."

"Well," said Mouse after thinking quietly for a few minutes, "if I could be anything, I'd be a wizard, so I could do really neat tricks."

"Well, you just did a really neat trick," Badger pointed out.

"You really think it was neat?" Mouse asked hopefully.

"Absolutely!" Badger insisted. "C'mon. Let's go back to our den and see if we can make you a wizard's costume!"

Raccoon always had her pumpkin party in the deserted barn at the edge of the forest, and she always had it late in the afternoon. Everyone had to bring some kind of food and, if they wanted, a carved pumpkin. Badger and Fox brought theirs in a wagon they borrowed from the Porcupine Twins. On the way they stopped to get Mouse. She looked great in her wizard's costume – gown, cape, and tall, pointy hat.

By the time the three of them arrived, many of their friends were already there. Inside the barn they found a ballerina, a pirate, Peter Rabbit, Puss in Boots, a butterfly, a Blue Fairy, a kangaroo, two aliens, a bumblebee, and a friendly monster. Several old wooden tables were covered with bowls of fruit and nuts, and plates of muffins, cakes, and cookies. All around the barn stood pumpkins with scary faces.

But there were other scary things as well. Spiders had woven big webs on the posts and beams, and a group of Bat's friends hung from the ceiling making clicking sounds. Owl, hidden somewhere in the shadows, called "Hoo! Hoo! Hoo!" over and over until – without warning – he broke into a series of barks, shrieks, hisses, and cries that made everyone shudder.

Still, the barn was a great place to play hide and seek, and Mouse was an expert at this game. She could squeeze into corners some of the bigger animals could barely see, and several times no one at all could find her. She was also very good at playing treasure hunt, and when the animals formed treasure-hunting teams, everyone wanted Mouse on their team. This made her very, very happy.

When at last it got too dark to hunt for treasures, Raccoon suggested they bob for apples. At one end of the barn stood a trough of water fed by a spring. Beaver, Woodchuck, and Rabbit helped push a bench next to it, and Raccoon set ten apples bobbing in the water. The darker it got, the brighter glowed the faces of the pumpkins. Some looked fierce, some angry, some a little goofy. One, however, smiled a mysterious smile.

❖

Suddenly a Porcupine Twin saw something and froze. He pointed, and the other animals turned to look. One of the pumpkins – the one with the mysterious smile – seemed to be winking at them! Everyone stared in amazement. Some gasped and some rubbed their eyes. Some shook their heads in disbelief. The big dark barn fell completely still – as though cast under a spell.

Then they head a laugh – a sharp little laugh – hee-hee-hee-hee, hee-hee-hee-hee-hee. But before anyone could scream or run away – presto! – the top of the pumpkin flew off and who should pop up but Mouse – Mouse, the wonderful wizard! "Hey, guys," she called out, "it's me, Mouse. I hope I didn't scare you too much. I hope you liked my little trick! Was it spooky enough?" Everyone let out a big sigh of relief.

It wasn't hard to decide: the pumpkin brought by Badger, Fox, and Mouse definitely deserved the scariest pumpkin prize. But Badger and Fox insisted it was really Mouse who should get the prize because the trick was her idea. It was she who suggested, if they used a flashlight instead of a candle to light their pumpkin, she could sneak inside and make it wink. It was also her idea to add the eerie little laugh.

By now it was quite dark outside, but by the light of the glowing pumpkins they could all see the prize Mouse had won: a big loaf of Raccoon's famous pumpkin bread.

Mouse, of course, wanted to share it. So, after slicing it up, she passed pieces around for all to enjoy. "See," said Fox, taking her piece, "with a good costume, you can be anything you want!"

The Strange Signs

"Hey, Fox," Badger called, "come look at this." Fox let go of the branch she was swinging on and came over to see what Badger was pointing to. "What do you make of that?" Badger asked.

"Hmm!" Fox puzzled. "Do you think it's a paw print?"

"If it is," Badger frowned, "it's the biggest paw print I ever saw."

"Let's see what else we can find," Fox suggested.

A few minutes later Fox called out, "Hey, Badger, look over here. All the branches are broken and the grass is trampled. Something must have pushed through these bushes." Then, after following a trail of broken branches and trampled grass, the two friends came upon what was clearly a paw print.

"Where there's one, there must be others," Badger figured. "Let's see if we can find them."

Soon they discovered an entire set of tracks that seemed to be coming from the river, near where Otter had his den. When they reached the river bank, the tracks disappeared. Badger knocked on Otter's door.

"Hi, Otter," Badger said when Otter opened, "we've just found some strange tracks in the forest, and they seem to come from the river. Do you know anything about them? Have you seen any new animals around here?"

"Well," Otter replied, "funny you should ask. I haven't seen any strange tracks or new animals, but…you know, a few days ago while I was napping, I thought I heard a loud ripping sound – like a big piece of wood being pulled apart. Why don't we go see if we can find it? Maybe the sound and the tracks are connected."

"Good idea," said Fox, and she, Badger, and Otter started searching the river bank for something that might have made the noise Otter heard.

It didn't take long to find it. Right beside the river lay a rotten log that had recently been torn open. They could tell because there were jagged pieces of wood scattered all around on the trampled grass. They also found many more tracks. "I guess this is what I heard," Otter decided. "Some animal was pulling this log apart."

"And look here," Badger said, pointing to one of the bigger pieces of log. "It looks like something has been scratched into the wood. – Maybe it's a message."

"Can you tell what it says?" Fox asked.

"I'm not sure," Badger replied, studying the scratch marks from different angles. "I'm not even sure it's writing, but if it is, I think it says "BEAR'S RIVER.""

"Then those must be bear tracks," Otter concluded with a little shudder. "Bear tracks," Badger repeated, putting down the piece of log.

"C'mon," cried Fox, "Now that we know what they are and where they come from, let's find out where they go."

"Right," said Badger slowly. "We do need to find out where they go."

And with that the three friends returned the way Badger and Fox had come and began following the tracks in the other direction.

Eventually they led close to where Raccoon lived. "Let's ask Raccoon if she knows anything," Badger suggested. "Hi, Raccoon," she said when Raccoon came to the door, "We've just been following some strange tracks up from the river and they seem to lead this way. Have there been any new animals around here?"

"That's very interesting," Raccoon answered. "Yesterday I thought I heard a grunting and snorting I'd never heard before, but when I came out and looked around, I didn't see anything."

"Look!" Otter suddenly cried, pointing to the smooth grey bark of a big beech tree. Everyone turned to look, and what they saw was unmistakable. Someone had scratched into the bark a set of rough letters. Badger went up close and read out loud: "BEAR'S FOREST."

"Hmm," said Raccoon, coming up and standing beside Badger. "Does that mean what I think it means?"

"Right," said Badger. "We definitely have a bear in the forest."

"So what do we do now?" Otter asked.

"I guess we have to find it and ask it what it's doing here," Badger suggested.

"And learn what all those messages mean," Fox added.

"They don't seem very friendly to me," Otter frowned.

"I guess we'll find out," Fox shrugged. "Let's see where the tracks lead next."

They led to a hilly area near Woodchuck's den – and they were now everywhere – as though the animal that made them was crisscrossing back and forth looking for something. When they came to Woodchuck's den, Woodchuck was standing outside, looking at his door. It was hanging by a single hinge, and the doorframe had been bent out of shape.

"Woodchuck! What happened?" Badger called in alarm.

"I don't know," Woodchuck said, shaking his head. "I was out taking a walk and when I got home a few minutes ago, this is what I found."

The five friends gathered around the entrance to the den, examining the damage. "It looks like someone too big for the door was trying to push their way in," Woodchuck noted. "Who could have done that?" The others all looked at each other and said at the same time, "a bear!"

"A bear?" Woodchuck asked, but before anyone could explain, they heard a rustling of leaves and a snapping of twigs as if something big was making its way through the bushes behind them. A second later out stepped a bear!

❖

The bear seemed as startled by the smaller animals as they were by it. It stopped and took a little step backwards. "Hi," called Fox, the first one to find her voice. "You must be new here. Welcome to our forest."

The bear wasn't that big – as bears go – but it wasn't that small either.

"Welcome to *your* forest?" the bear growled but still looked a bit confused. "What do you mean *your* forest?" he growled again. "I'm the biggest and the strongest, so it's *my* forest," and he growled a third time.

❖

"What a funny idea," said Badger with a little laugh. "What makes you think 'biggest and strongest' means more than…" she paused to think.

But before she could continue, Fox continued for

117

her, "means more than 'biggest and strongest.' Like I'm the fastest runner means I'm the fastest runner, and Badger's the best organizer means she's the best organizer, just as Otter, Raccoon, and Woodchuck are the best whatever, and – well – everyone's the most or the best something – or could be – and that's all it means!"

"Exactly," said Badger, looking at Fox with a big smile. "So, you see, the forest belongs to all of us, and that can include you too if you want to live here." The others nodded in agreement, but the bear still said nothing, as if the idea of sharing a forest were the most amazing thing he had ever heard of.

Then Woodchuck spoke up. "I bet you're looking for a winter den to sleep in, right?"

The bear again looked amazed and asked, "How did you know that?"

"Because," Woodchuck answered, "I also like to sleep through the winter, and I'd invite you to share my den, but, as you already know, it's not big enough." Woodchuck and the bear both looked at the broken door. The bear seemed a bit embarrassed.

"Wait a minute," Badger said brightly. "I have an idea! Why couldn't Bear sleep in the cave we use as a

clubhouse? It's dry and plenty big enough for a bear
– and I bet we won't want to use it again till spring."

"That's a great idea!" said Fox.

"Terrific!" agreed Woodchuck, "And maybe in the
spring Bear will even want to join our club!" Bear
looked very pleased at this turn in the conversation,
and for the first time he smiled.

"Hey, Bear," Fox winked, "maybe in the spring I can
show you where the best berries grow."

"And maybe you'd like to know about some great
fishing spots," Raccoon shrugged.

"And when it gets really hot, I can take you to the
coolest pool in the river," chimed in Otter.

By now Bear had a really big grin on his face. Finally,
after shuffling his feet a little, he said, "I can't believe
how lucky I am I found this forest – and so many new
friends."

"We're also lucky we met you," laughed Fox.
"It wouldn't be much fun to have a grumpy bear
wandering around. – After all, you are the biggest and
the strongest!"

The Beautiful Night

"Hey, Badger," Fox asked one evening after supper, "Do you know where I put my winter shoes?"

"Good question," Badger answered. "Do you remember when you last wanted to find them?"

"I bet it was sometime last winter, right?"

"You're exactly right. When we first decided to share the same den."

"So," Fox continued, "do you know where my shoes are this winter?"

Badger got out the box where they kept their winter stuff – shoes and hats and scarves and mittens – and found Fox's winter shoes. "Are you going for a walk?" she asked. "It's pretty late."

"That's okay. As long as it's not too cold," Fox replied.

"Then I think I'll go with you," Badger said. "But first

I have a special treat." And without another word, she took out of the cupboard a big pan. "Your favorite," she smiled, "triple chocolate fudge brownies."

Fox was so excited, her whiskers began to twitch. Suddenly she announced, "And I made something for you!"

"You did?" Badger asked in surprise.

"I did," Fox nodded, going to get her guitar. "It may sound a little like the Sunshine song, but I just made it up – just for you." Then she sang:

> *You are my best friend, my very best friend,*
> *You always help me to find my shoes,*
> *I'd give up candy to have you handy,*
> *There are so many things that I lose.*

"You're right," Badger said. "It is sort of like the Sunshine song but," she added, "it's still very special. Thank you." And she blushed a little.

"Glad you like it," Fox grinned. "Now let's have a brownie before we go for our walk."

So Badger cut each of them a brownie and poured two glasses of milk. "Yummm," Fox closed her eyes as she ate hers, "These are so delicious. How could anyone not love them? – Hey, I have a great idea!"

"Is it about another song?" Badger asked.

"No, it's about the brownies," Fox answered. "Since we're going for a walk, why don't we bring some to our friends?"

"Fox," Badger looked amazed, "you mean you'd share your favorite, your all-time-favorite fox treat with our friends?"

"Sure," said Fox, "as long as we keep plenty for me – I mean, for us."

"But many of our friends have already gone to sleep," Badger pointed out.

"That's okay," Fox nodded. "We don't have to wake anyone. We can just surprise them by leaving brownies outside their door. Then, when they go out in the morning, they'll find them and wonder who left them. We can even pretend we got some too!"

"That sounds like fun," Badger agreed and then added, "What a great way to celebrate a year of friendship!"

☆

So they got to work. Badger cut the brownies while Fox cut squares of aluminum foil to wrap them in. While Fox tied a white ribbon around each present, Badger slipped under the ribbon a little piece of paper with the word ENJOY written on it. Then they put the presents in a basket, pulled on their winter shoes, their jackets, their scarves and hats, and went out.

It was a beautiful night – crisp but not too cold. The moon was already high in the sky. Somewhere in the distance Owl was hooting softly, and a breeze gently shook the dry leaves still hanging from the oaks and beeches. In the moonlight, familiar shapes – trees and bushes and boulders – greeted them like shadowy friends.

Since Badger and Fox knew by heart the paths around their den, they had no trouble finding their way. They went first to Rabbit's burrow. All was perfectly still. Badger took one of the brownie packets from the basket, and put it by his door. The aluminum foil flashed in the moonlight. "That's really neat," Fox whispered and took out another packet to see how many different ways she could make it flash. Then she put it back, and they moved on.

The next stop was Raccoon's den. "We have to be especially quiet," Badger warned. "Raccoon likes to stay up late." And, sure enough, as they approached her den, they could see a bar of light beneath her door. "Wait here," Badger said, as she took a brownie packet

and handed the basket to Fox. Walking on tiptoe, she
approached the den and placed the present on the door
sill.

From Raccoon's den they went to Squirrel's, which
was in a hollow tree. Everyone knew Squirrel liked to
go to bed early, so they were pretty sure she wouldn't
be up. In less than a minute Fox had scrambled up
the tree and left a present wedged between two
branches. Then she and Badger again moved on –
first to Mouse's place and afterwards to Possum's and
Otter's. Finally Fox scrambled up Owl's tree and also
left him a present.

They were now just about finished. They couldn't leave a present for Beaver – because the door to his lodge was underwater. And they didn't leave one for Woodchuck because he was already asleep for the winter. So were Bear, Turtle, and Snake. Skunk and the Porcupine Twins now slept for many days at a time, but since they still occasionally got up to eat, they also got brownies.

"That was fun!" Badger said, swinging the empty basket on her arm.

"But wouldn't it be even more fun if we could see their faces when they find their presents?" Fox added.

"I can't wait to hear who they think left them," Badger giggled. "Try hard not to give away our secret."

"I'll try," Fox promised, "but I never know when something will just pop out of my mouth without asking."

On their way home the two friends came to a big meadow. The moon had now set, and there were no lights anywhere in the forest. As they moved away from under the branches of the trees, they both stopped in amazement. Never had they seen so many stars! "Wow, said Badger, "There must be millions of them."

"Yeah," said Fox, "like the time I knocked over a bowl of sugar."

"I read somewhere that the sky is full of animal pictures," Badger explained quietly, "like a bear and a snake and a rabbit – maybe even a fox and a badger. You just have to connect certain stars."

Fox stared at the sky with a puzzled look. "Which stars? There are too many to connect. – But if I close my eyes, I can see lots of things – like triple fudge chocolate brownies and plump red raspberries and …"

All at once, Badger grabbed Fox's arm. "Look!" she cried, "a shooting star…and, look, there's another – and another!"

"Where?" Fox asked, then immediately answered her own question, "Oh, over there and there and there…" And indeed the sky was now alive with streaks of light. Four, five, six at a time – they raced across the starry night like messengers in the darkness. For perhaps ten minutes shooting stars filled the sky from horizon to horizon – and then they were gone.

Fox turned to Badger. "What do you think happens to them when they disappear?" she asked. "Do you think they land in a forest somewhere?"

"No, I don't think so," Badger answered. "I think they just – they just disappear, like a match that gets blown out."

"That's kind of sad," Fox decided.

"It is," Badger agreed. "But maybe they would be happy to know someone saw them while they were here and thought they were wonderful."

Fox looked at Badger, Badger at Fox, and they gave each other a hug. Then they continued walking home. "It feels like we've been away a long time," Badger said as they approached the entrance to their den. "Did you ever expect the night to be so beautiful?" she added, almost to herself.

"Before I brush my teeth, I think I'll have one more, tiny piece of brownie," Fox answered.

It took a very long time for them to go to sleep. Instead, they lay in their beds talking about their friends and the presents they had left for them and the friends they would see in the spring. When they finally did turn off the light and close their eyes, they saw again the shooting stars that had filled the night sky. "Good night, Fox," Badger whispered, but Fox was already asleep.

About the Author . . .

Edward Zlotkowski has long had a special interest in children's literature. After a career as a Professor of English, he became involved in a variety of early literacy programs for underserved children and has for several years served on the board of The Puppet Showplace, New England's premier puppet theater. *Badger and Fox* is his second children's book. In 2016 he published *What Jill Did While Jack Climbed the Beanstalk*, the second edition of which will appear in fall 2019.

More information about his publications as well as supplementary material for parents and educators based on the Badger and Fox stories can be found at **www.badgerandfoxandfriends.com.**

About the Illustrator . . .

Karen Busch Holman, is a fine artist and children's book illustrator living in Barrington, NH and Lafayette, New Jersey.

After her first children's book in 2001, *G is for Granite, A New Hampshire Alphabet* by Marie Harris, Karen found her calling. This is her 16th book with 6 more on the way for 2019/20.

Karen's work can also be found in numerous publications and books throughout New England. She is also the creator of the art that adorns every New Hampshire Heirloom Birth Certificate. She actively shares her love of art with elementary schools in the Northeast and New England.

For more information go to **karenbuschholman.com**.